# Hamlyn Favourite Fairy Stories in colour

Re-told by Lornie Leete-Hodge

Illustrated by Beverlie Manson

Hamlyn
London · New York · Sydney · Toronto

Published 1978 by
The Hamlyn Publishing Group Limited
London · New York · Sydney · Toronto
Astronaut House, Feltham, Middlesex, England
©Copyright The Hamlyn Publishing Group Limited 1978

ISBN 0 600 33671 9

Printed and bound in Spain
by Graficromo, S. A. - Córdoba

# Contents

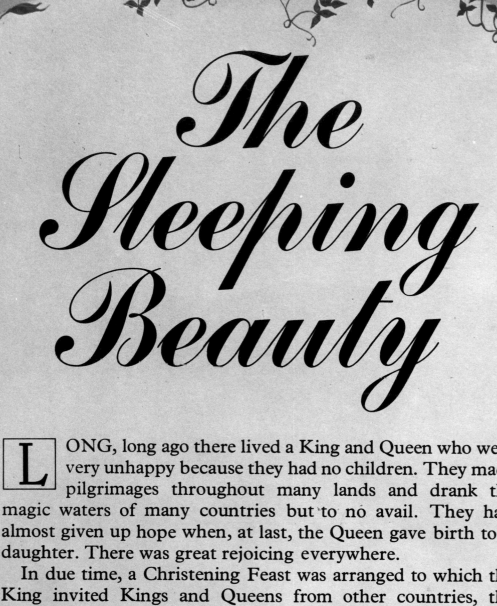

# The Sleeping Beauty

**L**ONG, long ago there lived a King and Queen who were very unhappy because they had no children. They made pilgrimages throughout many lands and drank the magic waters of many countries but to no avail. They had almost given up hope when, at last, the Queen gave birth to a daughter. There was great rejoicing everywhere.

In due time, a Christening Feast was arranged to which the King invited Kings and Queens from other countries, the nobles and ladies of his own kingdom, and as very special and honoured guests, the six fairies who lived in his realm. They would be the Princess's godmothers, and he hoped they would bestow magic gifts upon the child.

The banquet was prepared with places of honour for the six fairies. There was a golden table, spread with fine white linen and each fairy had a specially made golden casket containing a spoon, a fork and a knife made of gold and set with garnets, diamonds and rubies. No one had ever seen such fine presents before, but this was the Christening of a Princess.

The musicians played and everyone was sitting down to the feast when the door opened and a very old, very ugly fairy

8

entered leaning on a stick. She was dressed all in black and was very angry.

'You did not invite me!' she shrieked, waving her stick at the King and Queen.

'But, we, we . . .' the King stammered. The truth was that no one had seen the fairy for so long, they all thought she was dead, and they had forgotten all about her.

Hastily, the King ordered that a place be prepared for her with the other fairies, but, of course, there was no golden casket or knife, fork or spoon for her. The old fairy felt she had been slighted and muttered threats and curses as she picked at the feast. One of the young fairies, who sat next to her, listened to her grumbling. She thought the old fairy might give the baby Princess an unlucky gift, so she hid behind some curtains. She hoped she would be the last to make her gift and would be able to mend any evil the old fairy might do.

One by one, the fairies came to the Princess to offer their gifts. The youngest wished that the child should be the most beautiful Princess in the whole world; the next that she should have the nature of an angel; the third that she should have grace and the fourth that she should dance to perfection. The fifth wished that she should sing like a nightingale.

Then it was the turn of the old fairy. Shaking with rage, and leaning heavily on her stick, she pointed a bony finger at the sleeping Princess and declared:

'One day, you will pierce your hand on a spindle and die!'

A shudder of horror ran through the company, and it was then the young fairy stepped from behind the curtains.

'Take heart,' she said to the weeping King and Queen, 'the Princess will not die. It is true that I have no power to break the evil fairy's spell, and your daughter will prick herself with a spindle when she is fifteen. But, instead of dying, she will fall into a very deep sleep that will last for a hundred years. When that time has passed, a King's son will come and wake her.'

The King, trying to avert the terrible fate decreed by the bad fairy, ordered that every spindle in the kingdom be destroyed. On pain of death, he forbade anyone to use a spinning wheel or keep a spindle in their homes. So all spinning ceased and the wheels were silent.

The years passed happily and the wicked fairy's decree was forgotten. One day, when the Princess was fifteen, she and her parents were visiting one of their castles in the country. The young Princess was running about, exploring all the rooms, for she had never been there before. It was all a new adventure for her and she laughed as she ran from place to place.

At last she saw a tiny, twisting stairway that led up to a small garret at the top of the tower. Quickly, she ran up the stairs and stopped outside a door. She could hear a strange, whirring sound. Inside, an old woman sat spinning. She had not heard the King's orders forbidding the use of spinning wheels.

'Oh, what are you doing?' asked the Princess, coming into the room and watching the old woman.

'I am spinning, child,' said the old woman. She did not recognise the Princess.

'Oh, what is that?' asked the Princess, 'no one has told me of such a thing. How do you do it? Please let me try.'

The old woman handed her the spindle. No sooner had she picked it up, than she pricked her hand and fell into a deep sleep.

The old woman was very alarmed. She cried out for help and people came running from all over the castle. They threw water on the Princess's face, they rubbed her hands, they undid her clothes and even bathed her face with sweet-smelling perfume. But it was all to no avail. Nothing would waken her and she continued to sleep.

14

The King and Queen hurried back to their home, taking the sleeping Princess with them. The King ordered that she be placed in her bedchamber, on a bed embroidered with gold and silver.

The Princess looked beautiful lying asleep on her bed. Her sleep had not taken the colour from her cheeks which were pink and her lips were a pale coral. Although her eyes were closed, she still breathed gently, so they knew she was not dead. Her father ordered that she be left to sleep quietly until the spell be broken.

16

The good fairy, who had saved the life of the Princess by putting her to sleep, was out of the kingdom when the evil fairy's spell came true. A little dwarf, wearing seven league boots, came to tell her and she rode at once to the castle in a fiery chariot drawn by dragons.

'Everything is just right,' she said, looking round and trying to comfort the King and Queen. Then she suddenly thought that the Princess would feel lonely when she woke up and she picked up her magic wand. Gently, she tapped everyone in the castle—all the ladies and gentlemen of the court, the governesses, the officers, the stewards, the pages, the footmen, the guards, even the cooks, scullions, pantry boys and gardeners. Outside, she touched all the fine horses in the stable, the great watchdogs and little Mopsey, the Princess's pet dog. He climbed on to his mistress's bed and curled up at the foot of it.

Everyone fell asleep at once. The whole castle was silent, even the logs on the fire stopped burning and the chickens turning on the spits were still. The King and Queen kissed their daughter and the fairy touched them with her wand.

17

A great silence fell; time stood still. Within a few minutes of the enchantment, a great forest of enormous trees with bushes and briars sprang up all round the castle hiding it from sight. So no one would see the sleeping Princess until it was time for the spell to be broken.

A hundred years passed. One day the son of the reigning King (for a different family ruled the kingdom) was out hunting. He asked what the towers were he could just see peeping out of a great wood.

'It's a ruined old castle,' said one courtier.

'It's the home of an ogre who steals children,' said another. The Prince did not know what to think until he asked a very old peasant.

'Your Highness,' he said, 'more than fifty years ago, I heard my father tell that the most beautiful Princess in the world lies in that castle. She must sleep for a hundred years and only a King's son can wake her.'

The young Prince was filled with excitement. He had to see if the legend were true and if there really was a beautiful Princess asleep in the castle. Picking up his sword, he began to cut a way through the forest of trees, bushes and briars, but scarcely had he begun to do so, than they parted for him and the way was clear. Alone he rode on to the castle and came to the great forecourt. Looking about, he was filled with an icy terror. There was a terrible silence and the face of death all around him. Men, women and animals all appeared to be dead. It was very strange, for even the cups they held were filled with wine, and not a drop had spilt.

Bravely, the Prince pushed open the great door and climbed up a wide staircase. Here, everyone was fast asleep. Every room was the same. At last, he came to a room lined with gold. The curtains of the bed were pulled back and, lying on a bed embroidered with gold and silver, was the most beautiful girl he had ever seen. At the foot of the bed, a small dog slept peacefully.

The Prince put out his hand and touched her face, but she did not move.

'Do wake up,' he whispered and fell on his knees by the bed.

Just then, the enchantment ended, and the Princess fluttered her eyelids. 'Is that you my Prince?' she asked, 'I have waited a long time.'

The Prince was delighted, and bent and kissed her, and told her he loved her. Then, the spell was completely broken at last and everyone in the castle woke up and there was a great noise. The dogs barked, the horses neighed and the people chattered such as you have never heard before.

The King and Queen came to greet their daughter and saw that the fairy's words had come true. A Prince had woken her from her enchanted sleep.

Life at the castle went on as if it had not stopped for a hundred years. In the kitchen, the cook cuffed the kitchen boy for not turning the spit fast enough and the musicians played, the music sweeter than it had ever sounded before.

The Prince and Princess were married in the castle chapel and lived happily ever after.

# Cinderella

ONCE upon a time there lived a rich merchant whose wife had died leaving him all alone with his pretty daughter. So he married a widow with two daughters of her own, hoping that they would be friends with his own child. But he was mistaken. His new wife was the most snobbish and bad tempered woman in the land, who cared for no one but her own two daughters who were plain and spiteful.

She was soon jealous of the merchant's daughter who was sweet and kind, and made her do all the housework. From morn till night, the girl toiled in the great house, sweeping and dusting, polishing and cleaning, till the place sparkled.

Her stepsisters lay in bed, while she waited on them, or else they preened themselves in front of the mirrors that shone with polishing. It was 'fetch this' or 'bring that' all day long, until, when the evening came, she was glad to curl up in the embers of the fire to keep warm.

The poor girl bore it all with patience. Soon her clothes turned into rags, but even with her cheeks stained with tears and soot from the fire, she was ten times prettier than her two ugly stepsisters. From her habit of sitting in the fireplace her

22

stepsisters called her Clinkerlump, but the younger sister, who wasn't *quite* so unkind, sometimes called her Cinderella.

So the days passed and while the stepsisters grumbled and groused, for nothing was ever right for them, Cinderella still smiled as she worked.

One day there was great excitement in the merchant's house. A herald from the castle brought them an invitation to a grand ball which the King was giving in honour of his son's birthday. All the nobility and people of importance from round and about were to be invited, including the stepsisters because they were rich and well known.

24

They were very happy and excited at the thought of going to the castle and meeting the Prince who was known to be very handsome. All day long they looked at fine materials, and the bundles of silks, satins and rich velvets lay all round the house until the merchant began to grumble at the sight of them. But still the stepsisters could not make up their minds! Everything had to be right for this special occasion. Cinderella had excellent taste so her sisters asked her advice, which she gave freely.

At last the elder sister made up her mind. 'I shall wear red velvet with a lace trimming,' she announced, 'and I must have new red shoes to match.'

'Well, I shall wear a silk skirt with a gold-flowered cloak,' said her sister, 'and my diamond necklace will be just right.'

25

26

So the dressmakers and shoemakers were called in and the needles flew. At last the dresses were ready and Cinderella thought they were beautiful. But they did not please the sisters, who found fault with them, and she had to alter this, and sew that until they were satisfied.

On the day of the ball, Cinderella ran from one to the other helping them into their finery. The hairdressers came and piled their hair on top of their heads in the fashion of the day, while the sisters complained that this curl was too long, or this one too short. In the end, it was Cinderella who brushed and smoothed their hair to their satisfaction, and at last they were ready. They looked magnificent.

The younger sister, taking a last look in the mirror, said, 'Wouldn't you like to go to the ball, Cinderella?'

'Don't laugh at me,' begged Cinderella, 'I have no place there.'

'Yes, that's true,' said her cruel sister, 'everyone would laugh to see a Clinkerlump at the ball!'

Cinderella hung her head and said nothing. She helped them into their carriage, laughing and excited, and watched them out of sight down the road to the castle. Then she returned to the kitchen, and, sitting among the embers of the fire, she began to cry.

All at once there was a sudden light in the room! Startled, Cinderella looked up. Then she saw a shining figure standing beside her, glowing and beautiful.

'Don't be afraid, child,' the lady said gently. 'I am your fairy godmother. Why are you crying?'

'I should like . . . Oh, what's the use?' said Cinderella and could not stop her tears.

'You want to go to the ball, don't you?' asked her fairy godmother.

'Yes, yes,' sobbed Cinderella.

'Very well, so you shall!' said her fairy godmother. 'Do just as I tell you. Go into the garden and bring me the biggest pumpkin you can find.'

Drying her eyes, Cinderella went out and cut the largest pumpkin in the patch and brought it to her godmother. She could not see how a pumpkin would get her to the ball, but she watched as her godmother scraped all the seeds out, then touched it with her magic wand. It turned into a golden coach!

'Good, now for the horses to pull it,' said her godmother. 'If you look in the mousetraps, you will find six white mice. Bring them to me.'

As she was bid, Cinderella found the mousetraps. There were six white mice which she gave to her godmother. As the trap was gently lifted and each mouse ran out, she touched it with her magic wand and it turned into a prancing horse. Soon, there was a team of six white horses in front of the coach.

'Now for the coachman,' ordered her godmother. 'Go and look in the rat trap.'

The rat trap held a large, fat rat with fine whiskers. With a tap of the wand, it was transformed into a splendid coachman with twinkling eyes and the best whiskers you have ever seen.

'All we need now are the footmen,' said Godmother. 'In the garden shed, hiding by the watering can, you will see six lizards. Bring them to me.'

28

Cinderella was too happy to argue and soon the lizards turned into six footmen with snow-white breeches and blue velvet coats. They looked magnificent, just as if they had been born footmen.

'Well, there you are,' said the fairy godmother, 'you can go to the ball. Hurry up and get ready.'

'But how can I go in these rags?' asked Cinderella, holding out her tattered skirt.

Laughing, the fairy godmother touched Cinderella gently with her wand. At once the rags fell away and Cinderella was wearing a beautiful dress of gold and silver that sparkled as she moved. There was a necklace of diamonds in her hair to catch the light. Cinderella could not believe her eyes – this was truly a magic dress.

'Here are the slippers,' said her godmother holding out the daintiest, prettiest pair of glass slippers in the world. Cinderella gasped. 'Is this really happening?' she asked.

'Of course, now hurry along and enjoy yourself,' said her godmother kissing her, 'but whatever you do, do not stay after midnight. My magic will not last after then and everything will be as before. As soon as the clock strikes, you will be in rags.'

'I'll remember,' promised Cinderella and climbed into her coach.

The night was alive with stars which twinkled like tiny lights, and as the coach approached the castle on the hilltop, Cinderella could hear the faint echo of music and see the flickering shadows cast by the lanterns that swung from the walls.

When the Prince heard that a great and beautiful Princess had arrived in a magnificent coach, he came to greet her and led her to the ballroom. The music stopped and everyone stared at Cinderella. No one had ever seen anyone so beautiful. 'Who is she?' they whispered among themselves, but no one knew the answer.

Cinderella danced with the Prince, who could not take his eyes off her and would dance with no one else. A magnificent supper was served, but the Prince ate nothing, he just wanted to gaze at his Princess. Cinderella sat near her sisters and even offered them a dish of tiny, sugared fruit, but they did not recognise her.

So the evening wore on and the Prince and Cinderella danced and danced to the music forgetting the time. Then she heard the first stroke of midnight. She made a deep curtsey to the King and Queen, and ran down the steps and out of the castle, heedless of the Prince's shouts for her to come back.

As she reached the last few steps she could hear the clock striking. 'Boom! Boom! Boom!' In her haste, she dropped one of her slippers, but dared not stop to pick it up. The clock stopped and Cinderella was once more in rags, the coach and horses gone, though she did see a large rat slinking away into the darkness. Swiftly, she ran home to await her sisters' return.

They could talk of nothing but the ball and the beautiful Princess who had danced with the Prince all evening!

At the castle, the Prince was desolate. No one had seen his Princess leave and the servants said they had seen only a kitchen maid in rags by the gates. He held the slipper in his hands. Somehow he must find his Princess. The King had an idea. 'Why not send the heralds out to seek the owner of the slipper?' he suggested, 'and then you will find the Princess.'

34

So the heralds went out into the land carrying the glass slipper. Every girl must try it on, and the Prince would marry the one who could wear it. Every house in the kingdom was visited and every woman tried on the slipper, but to no avail. On the third day, the Prince himself accompanied the heralds and they came at last to the merchant's house. The stepsisters tried to squeeze their feet into the tiny slipper. The elder, seeing her toe was too large, thought of cutting it off, but her sister, impatient for her try, snatched it just in time. The younger sister had no luck either, her heel stuck out by several inches!

'Is there anyone else in the house?' asked the heralds.

'Let me try,' said Cinderella, who had been watching in the background. Her sisters laughed and mocked her, but the Prince was insistent. Even in her rags, he could see she was beautiful.

Cinderella sat down and slipped her foot into the tiny slipper. It fitted her beautifully. The two sisters were astonished and could not believe their eyes, but Cinderella put her hand in her pocket and brought out the second slipper.

At that very moment, her fairy godmother arrived and, touching Cinderella with her wand, changed her rags once more into the magnificent ball dress she had worn at the Castle.

The two sisters recognised the Princess and begged her forgiveness, and Cinderella kissed them and took them to the castle with her.

The Prince was overjoyed. He had found his Princess. In a few days they were married and lived happily ever after.

37

# Puss in Boots

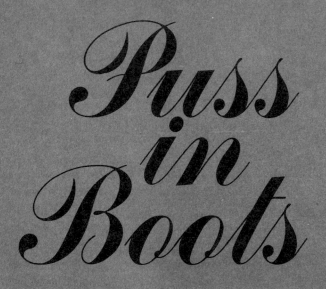

ONCE upon a time there was a poor miller who had three sons. When he died, he left his mill to the eldest son, his donkey to the second son, and his cat to the youngest son, Tom.

Tom was very sad for he knew that his brothers could go into partnership and use the donkey to work the mill, but he felt that he had nothing. 'Maybe I could kill the cat and sell its fur,' he said. The cat overheard Tom and cried, 'don't kill me, just give me what I ask and I will make your fortune!'

Tom was very surprised. 'What do you want?' he asked.

'I'd like a pair of high boots – red leather, I think,' said Puss, 'and a sack, and, if you can manage it, a hat with a feather.'

Tom laughed but he had nothing to lose, so he asked the shoemaker to make a fine pair of red leather boots for Puss. The cat was so pleased with the boots that he wore them all the time. Everyone called him Puss in Boots. Tom found him a hat and a sack as well.

Next day, the cat put on his new blue hat with a long white feather, and, picking up his bag, went out into the fields. He put some lettuce and bran in the sack, then hid out of sight. It was not long before two silly rabbits found the food and Puss snared them in no time.

Tossing his catch over his shoulder, Puss in Boots set off for the King's palace. He demanded to see the King at once and bowed low before His Majesty.

'Your Majesty,' he said, 'I bring you a gift from my master, the Marquis of Carabas.' And he gave the plump, juicy rabbits to the King.

For a week, the cat took presents of fish and game to the King and told him they were all gifts from the Marquis of Carabas, his master. Then one morning, by listening to all the talk at Court, Puss learned that the King and his beautiful daughter were going for a drive beside the river the next day. Puss quickly worked out a plan to help his master. He ran back to Tom and told him to do exactly as he said.

'Go and bathe in the river tomorrow afternoon, and leave the rest to me.'

So, next day, Tom was swimming in the river when he heard coach wheels coming along the road. Puss was there and he ran out to stop the coach.

'Help! Help!' he cried, 'my master, the Marquis of Carabas is drowning!'

The King ordered the coach to stop and his footmen helped Tom out of the water. 'Someone has stolen his clothes,' wailed Puss, so the King ordered that a suit be brought from the palace. In fact, crafty Puss had hidden Tom's clothes under a stone!

Meanwhile, Puss had come to a fine castle on a hill. A fierce ogre lived here, and everyone was afraid of him. In fact, it was he who really owned all the lands that the King was driving through. Puss in Boots asked to see him and told him that the King was on his way and was looking forward to meeting so great a land-owner.

The ogre was very flattered and asked Puss to sit down.

'I have heard so much about you,' said Puss, 'but I am sure it is all lies.'

Hearing this, the ogre became very angry. 'Who dares to tell lies about me?' he bellowed. 'Tell me what they say, tell me who they are, and I shall have them cut into tiny pieces!'

Truth to tell, Puss was a little scared, but there was no going back now.

'They say,' he went on, leaning forward and speaking softly, 'that you can turn yourself into a lion. But I don't believe that rubbish,' he said, twirling his hat.

'Rubbish is it?' the ogre shouted, jumping to his feet. 'I can do anything!' With that, he turned himself into a fierce lion which roared most dreadfully.

Puss made himself sit still. After all, a lion was only a big cat, he told himself, a member of his own family!

'Very good,' he said, 'but is it true that you can turn yourself into a small animal – a mouse for instance?'

The lion gave a low growl.

'There, I knew it was impossible,' said Puss, 'they do tell lies about you!'

'Nothing is impossible for me,' roared the ogre, and still raging, he changed himself into a mouse. Puss caught him with one pounce and ate him up. Dusting his whiskers, he ran to the courtyard to greet the King for he had heard the coach clattering in.

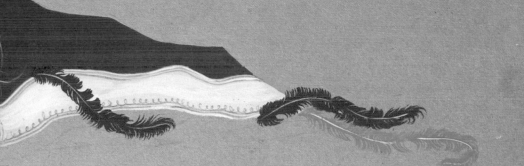

'Welcome to the castle of the Marquis of Carabas!' he said bowing low.

The King and Princess were delighted that the Marquis lived in such a fine castle, and Tom liked it too.

'Dinner is served,' said Puss and they all sat down to a great feast which had been prepared for the ogre.

Tom asked the King for the Princess's hand in marriage, and the King was very happy to let his daughter marry such a rich and handsome young man. They lived very happily at the castle for many years but Tom never told the Princess that Puss in Boots had made him the Marquis of Carabas, for that was their secret! Puss had kept his promise and Tom was rich and happy.

As for Puss in Boots, he lived in the castle too, but he never tried to catch another mouse. The taste of the ogre had been too horrible!

Aladdin ran home to tell his mother about the stranger and she was very surprised for she did not know that her husband had had a brother. But she prepared a meal for the stranger and welcomed him to her house.

The truth was that the stranger was not Aladdin's uncle at all, but a wicked magician. The magician had seen Aladdin playing in the streets all day and decided he would use this lazy, foolish boy to help him.

The magician told Aladdin's mother that he had been away for many years and had just returned from Africa.

'I will look after you,' he said, 'you will never go hungry again.'

Before he left, he gave Aladdin's mother some gold and told her to buy wine and food to celebrate his return. He promised that he would rent a market stall for Aladdin and help him by stocking it with merchandise.

Next day, the magician took Aladdin to the finest shops and bought him magnificent clothes. Then, as evening fell, he led him to a beautiful garden outside the town. Fountains played and the scent from the brightly-coloured flowers hung heavy on the air.

They looked at the fountains and the flowers and then went on to another even finer garden, and then another and another until they came at last to a deep valley with mountains on either side. The magician told Aladdin to fetch sticks for a fire. He set them alight and threw a few drops of oil on to the blaze. A thick, dense smoke curled round them. When it cleared, they could see a large, flat stone on the ground with a brass ring in the centre. Aladdin gasped in amazement and began to ask many questions, but the magician was in a hurry.

'Aladdin,' he said, holding his arm, 'you are the only person in the whole world who can move this stone. Underneath, you will see some steps that lead into a cave. Go through the cave and you will find a garden filled with priceless treasures. Take as much as you like, but bring me the lamp you will see burning on the terrace.'

Aladdin was afraid, though he liked the idea of the treasure. It all sounded very strange, but he was too scared and bewildered to refuse.

'One more thing,' said the magician, 'remember to pour the
the oil from the lamp before you bring it to me.'

He took a fine ring from his finger and gave it to Aladdin
saying that it would protect him from any evil.

So Aladdin did as he was told and lifted the stone. It was
exactly as the magician had said. He went down some steps and
through a cave until he came to a garden filled with such beauty
that Aladdin stood and stared in astonishment. He touched
the grass and found that each blade was a leaf of jade and the
flowers were diamonds, pearls and rubies that sparkled and

almost danced in the enchanted garden. Quickly, he gathered some jewels together and then he remembered the lamp. Just as the magician had said, the lamp stood, the flame burning steadily, on the wall of the terrace. Aladdin emptied the oil and put it away inside his coat with the jewels and hurried through the cave and up the steps.

The magician was waiting. 'Quickly boy, give me the lamp,' he cried, and tried to snatch it from Aladdin. This startled the boy and he fell back down the steps. The magician flew into a terrible rage. He threw more powder and oil on to the now smouldering fire and pushed the stone back into place, sealing Aladdin inside!

The magician's spells had shown him that this magic lamp would only work if it was given to him freely by another. He had thought Aladdin stupid enough to get it for him. But his plan had failed.

Aladdin was terrified and he cried out for help. For many hours he tried in vain to push back the stone, but it was far too heavy. It became very cold in the cave and he rubbed his hands together for warmth. As he did so he touched the magic ring he had been given. At once a huge genie stood in front of him, so large that it seemed to fill the whole cave.

The genie bowed low and said, 'I am the slave of the ring. What is your command, Master?'

'I want to go home,' said Aladdin, too surprised to be scared, and in a moment he was with his mother. She was overjoyed to see him and she was delighted with the jewels he had brought.

'I am so hungry,' said Aladdin, but his mother had nothing for him. 'I will sell this old lamp and buy something,' she said. She picked up some cotton and began to rub the lamp, for it was very dirty, and she thought it might fetch a better price if it was shining. At once an enormous genie appeared and asked her commands.

The poor woman was terrified and begged Aladdin to take the lamp from her. Aladdin picked up the lamp and ordered the genie to bring him some food.

The genie came back with a table laden with silver dishes and the finest food ever seen. But Aladdin's mother was still unhappy about the genie and begged him to part with the lamp and have nothing more to do with magic. Aladdin refused, and took the dishes to market where he sold them for so much money that they were never hungry again.

The years passed and the lamp lay forgotten. Then one day, Aladdin saw the Sultan's daughter being carried in a litter through the streets. She was so beautiful that he fell in love with her and wanted to marry her.

To show his love, he brought her the jewels he had taken from the garden and the Sultan was impressed for he knew their true value.

'Bring me forty times the number of jewels you have here and you may marry my daughter,' he promised.

Aladdin took the lamp and ordered the genie to bring him the jewels, and a magnificent horse for him to ride. He went to the palace on his fine horse, dressed in his best clothes, and with a long procession of slaves carrying all the jewels. The people in the streets looked on amazed.

The Sultan was delighted and at once agreed to the marriage. Aladdin rubbed his lamp again for he wanted a magnificent palace for his bride. Next morning the Sultan looked out of his window and was astonished to see a wonderful new palace opposite his own. No one had ever seen anything so beautiful and the wedding feast lasted for weeks.

Aladdin and his bride were very happy and the years passed quickly. One day, he was out hunting with his friends, when the magician returned to try once more to claim the lamp. He disguised himself as an old pedlar, and walked the streets with a tray of lamps crying, 'New lamps for old. New lamps for old.'

The Princess, who did not know the magic powers of Aladdin's lamp, wanted a bright new lamp, and called the pedlar to the palace. 'Here, take this,' she said and gave him the magic lamp.

The magician rubbed the lamp quickly, throwing the others to the ground. When the genie appeared, he commanded that the palace and the Princess be taken to his home in Africa. Aladdin came home to find everything had vanished. The Sultan was very angry and ordered his execution.

'Give me time to find the Princess,' Aladdin begged and the Sultan gave him forty days in which to bring her back.

Aladdin was in despair and he wrung his hands in misery. As he did so he accidentally rubbed the magic ring which he always wore, and once more the genie of the ring stood before him.

'Your wish is my command,' he said, and Aladdin asked him to take him to the Princess. 'I can take you to her prison,' said the genie, 'but you must rescue her yourself. I do not have the powers of the genie of the lamp.'

So Aladdin found himself transported to Africa, and he hid by the walls of his palace. He could see the Princess and called softly to her. She was very glad to see him again and told him that the magician treated her as a slave, and made her prepare all his food!

Aladdin gave his Princess a strong sleeping potion and told her to put it in the magician's dinner. When the magician had fallen into a deep sleep, the Princess signalled to Aladdin and he slipped into the palace and picked up his lamp. He commanded the genie of the lamp to take the sleeping magician to the ends of the earth and leave him there for ever!

'Now,' said Aladdin to the genie, 'take me and the Princess and the palace back to where we belong.'

When they were safely home, Aladdin ordered that a special case set with beautiful jewels, be made for the lamp. When it was ready, he placed it inside, and locked it up very securely. Then he hid the key, and no one has ever found it to this day. Meanwhile, the lamp burned bright in its jewelled hiding place, and Aladdin and his Princess lived happily ever after.

# The Golden Goose

THERE was once a woodcutter who lived with his wife and three sons in a small cottage on the edge of a great forest. The youngest boy was nicknamed 'Dummling' or 'Simpleton', because he was stupid. Everything he did turned out badly, no matter how he tried, and his brothers jeered at him all day long.

His parents were just the same. 'Our youngest is a fool and no mistake,' his mother would sigh, and give him a burnt piece of cake for his tea. Dummling never seemed to mind though, and was always happy and smiling.

One day the woodcutter had to cut down one of the very tallest fir trees growing in the forest. There it stood, its branches stretching out to the winds, the topmost ones reaching for the blue sky. But it had to come down all the same.

The eldest son said he would do the job for his father. His mother packed him a special lunch bag with some rich fruit cake she had just baked and a bottle of her best wine in case he felt thirsty.

He soon found the tree because his father had marked it with a big white cross. He took a look at it, but being a lazy boy,

decided to eat his lunch before cutting it down. He found a nice, shady bank and settled himself comfortably. The wine was cool and refreshing and he was soon tucking into a big slice of the cake. Then he saw a little, old, grey-bearded man coming along the path towards him.

'Good morning,' said the little man politely. 'I see you have a fine lunch, and it's a long time since I had a bite to eat or anything to drink. Will you share your cake and wine with me?'

'What an idea!' said the woodcutter's eldest son. 'Certainly not. I have never seen you before, I don't know you and I don't want to know you,' he added rudely. 'Besides, I need all the cake and wine for myself.'

The little old man looked at him hard for a moment, then he disappeared into the forest.

When the woodcutter's son took up his axe to cut down the tree, the axe slipped and cut his arm! The wound was so deep he had to give up work and return home. There he was fussed over by his mother, and he did not work again for weeks.

Then the woodcutter asked his second son to go and cut down the tree for him.

'Of course,' said the lad, full of confidence. 'I will take more care, and have the tree down in no time.'

His mother wrapped a fine, nutty cake for him that she had baked that morning, and gave him some wine to drink.

When the second son reached the tree, he took one glance and sat down to eat before beginning his task. He took out the cake and the wine, and was just about to start his meal when he saw a little, old, grey-bearded man coming along the path towards him.

'Good morning to you,' said the little man. 'Will you share your food with me? It's a very long time since I had a bite to eat or anything to drink.'

'Clear off,' said the second son rudely, 'I won't share my food with anyone. Be off with you!'

The little old man looked at him hard, then he disappeared into the forest, shaking his head as he went.

Soon, his meal finished, the second son began work on the tree. As he lifted the axe, he thought of the little old man. 'Fancy expecting me to give him some of my cake,' he said to himself, 'when I have finished this tree, I shall need ten cakes.' At first it was easy, and soon a pile of wood chips lay on the ground beside him. Then suddenly the axe slipped, cutting his leg so badly that he could scarcely drag himself home.

Dummling had watched his brothers go to the woods. He wanted to help his father, but knew that he would be laughed to scorn. Now was his chance!

'Father, let me try,' he begged, 'I am sure I can cut down the tree for you.'

'Well, your brothers could not do it, so I am sure you can't, but a day in the forest won't hurt you. You'll learn sense when you cut yourself – but don't cut your head off,' he added laughing.

Dummling was very pleased although his mother did not bake a special cake for him. 'There's a piece of bread on the shelf,' she said, 'and here's some beer to wash it down.'

Dummling set off down the path whistling to himself. He found the tree, and a little, old, grey-bearded man was standing beside it.

'Good morning,' the little man said, 'I see you have some food with you. Will you share it with a hungry old man who has not eaten for days?'

Dummling felt sorry for the old man. He *did* look tired and hungry. 'Of course, you are welcome to share my meal,' he said. 'But I am afraid it is not very much.'

Dummling broke the bread in half and offered the beer to the old man as they sat together on the bank in the sunshine.

Half an hour passed very happily, and Dummling discovered that the little man was full of fun. Their laughter rang through the forest, startling the birds, and making the deer pause from cropping and look at them.

Then the old man spoke. 'You have been kind to me, so I will help you. Don't cut down the tree marked with the cross, cut down that tree over there instead, and among its roots you will find something very valuable.'

With a smile and a wave, the little old man went off down the forest path. Dummling picked up his axe and walked over to the tree the old man had pointed out.

'Oh well, this one is as good as another,' he said, and swung his axe. After a few swift strokes, the blade flashing in the sunlight, the great tree came crashing to the ground, and its roots were pulled out of the earth to lie in a tangled heap on the grass. In the roots, to Dummling's open-mouthed astonishment, sat a goose with golden feathers!

Carefully and gently, he lifted the bird, stroking its feathers, and he realised they were of pure gold. This certainly was something valuable, too valuable to take home to his greedy brothers. He tucked the bird under his arm and set off for the nearest inn.

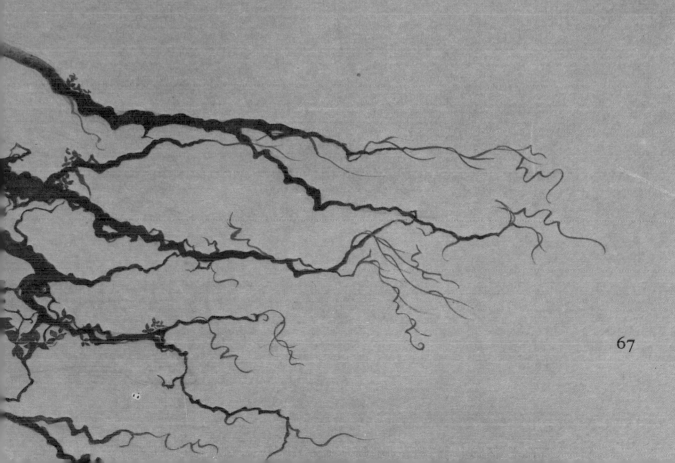

The innkeeper's daughters were full of curiosity as he showed them the goose, and told them that its feathers were golden.

'Oh, for just one of those feathers,' thought the eldest, and she planned how she might steal one.

The woodcutting and excitement had made Dummling tired, so tucking his goose gently on the end of the bed, he fell asleep. He did not hear the door creak open and the innkeeper's eldest daughter steal into the room. She was determined to have one of those lovely, golden feathers. Swiftly, she seized the goose's tail and pulled. But, imagine her surprise when she found that she could not move her hand! It was stuck fast to the goose and no matter how she tried, she could not move it.

The second daughter opened the door a crack and, like her sister, tried to snatch one of the gleaming feathers. But she, too, stuck firmly to the goose and no amount of pushing and pulling would free her.

At last the third daughter came to try her luck. But soon she joined her sisters and they all spent a very uncomfortable night in Dummling's room while he slept peacefully in his bed.

Next morning, Dummling picked up his goose without even looking, so he did not notice the three girls clinging to its feathers. He set off down the road at a brisk pace, whistling merrily and the poor girls had to run to keep up with him. When he stopped, they stopped, all bumping into each other, and when he turned right, they turned right. Wherever he went, they had

to follow. They cried out for help, and the parson, who was in his garden, hurried out to see what was the trouble. 'Shame on you!' he cried, thinking the girls were chasing Dummling, and he tried to pull them away. But he, too, was stuck fast and was soon running along behind the girls and Dummling. It was a very strange sight indeed.

As the little procession crossed the path in front of the church, the verger came running out, holding up his hands. 'Vicar, Vicar,' he cried, 'where are you going? Don't forget you have a Christening at noon.' And he took a firm grip on the parson's arm. He could not free himself, but, as he ran along behind the others, he called out to some men in a field.

'Help! Help! Do something!'

The men left their work and rushed up to the verger, but when they tried to pull him free, they, too, were stuck fast. No matter how they twisted and turned, and pulled and pushed, all seven of them were running along behind Dummling and his goose!

Without once looking back, for he was so happy, Dummling ran along the winding road, hopping and skipping and singing merrily to himself, while the luckless girls, the parson, the verger and the two farm men, hurried along behind.

At last they came to a beautiful city where the King lived in a fine castle. They could just see its battlements, with a flag flying from the topmost tower, as they hurried along. The King had a daughter of whom he was very fond, but she also made him very unhappy. She was so sad that she never, ever laughed. In desperation, the King had decreed that whoever made the Princess laugh or smile would win her hand in marriage.

At the castle gates was a large notice bearing this legend:

WHOEVER MAKES
THE KING'S DAUGHTER LAUGH
OR SMILE WINS HER HAND
IN MARRIAGE.

By Order of the King.

'How about that?' said Dummling to himself as he entered the city. 'So the Princess does not smile. I must see if I can cheer her up.'

The Princess was sitting by one of the castle windows as Dummling and his odd procession came through the gates. When she saw a young man, carrying a bright, golden goose under his arm and three girls, a parson, a verger and two farm workers in their smocks, trailing behind, all stuck fast, each to each, she burst out laughing. Dummling looked up and, seeing her, gave a cheery wave.

'It is a miracle,' cried the courtiers. 'The Princess is smiling, no, she is laughing! The King must be told.' And they ran to tell the King the good news.

Now the Princess was laughing so much, everyone thought she would never stop. The tears ran down her face, and all she could do was point to Dummling and his followers, and laugh and laugh and laugh.

'He is the winner,' cried the crowd, pushing Dummling forward. 'He made the Princess laugh, and he must marry her.' Everyone was laughing and cheering and waving.

Once inside the castle, the spell broke and the innkeeper's daughters, the parson, the verger and the two farm workers were all free. They all ran home before any more harm could befall them!

72

When the King saw Dummling he did not like the idea of letting him marry his daughter. After all, Dummling was only the son of a poor woodcutter, even if he had made the Princess happy.

So the King said that Dummling had to perform another task before he could win the Princess's hand.

'What is it?' asked Dummling.

'You must bring me someone who can drink a whole cellar full of wine,' said the King. 'That'll fix him,' he said to himself, rubbing his hands.

'I will see if I can find someone,' said Dummling and left the castle and went back to the forest. There, as he had hoped, the little old man was sitting on the tree stump.

'I have such a thirst,' the old man said, 'I could drink the sea dry, then all the rivers and all the streams.'

'Could you drink a cellar full of wine?' asked Dummling.

'A cellar full of wine!' laughed the little man, 'show me where it is. There is nothing better than wine when you are as thirsty as I am!'

So Dummling took the little old man back to the castle into the King's cellar which was brimming with wine. The casks of red and white wine were set in rows all along the walls, and Dummling did not think that anyone, especially anyone so small as his friend, could possibly drink it all.

When evening came, the old man had emptied every cask in the cellar. The King was very angry, because his trick had failed and now he had no wine left!

'All the wine is drunk,' said Dummling, 'and now I come to claim your daughter's hand in marriage.'

The King stroked his beard. He had another idea. 'There is another task to perform. Find me someone who can eat a mountain of bread.' And the King went away laughing.

Dummling returned to the tree in the forest and there, once again, he found the little, old, grey-bearded man. This time, he looked very sad and Dummling asked him what was troubling him.

'I am so hungry,' he sighed, 'that I think I could eat a mountain. I have eaten more than a hundred rolls already today, and look at my clothes, they hang on me like a sack.'

'Follow me,' said Dummling and took him back to the castle where, by the King's order, a mountain of bread was waiting. Dummling gasped at the pile of crispy, crunchy topped loaves, but the old man breathed in their smell with delight.

Hour after hour, the little man ate the bread and the mountain grew smaller and smaller until there was not one crumb left.

'The mountain of bread is eaten, not a crumb remains, so I have come to claim the Princess,' said Dummling to the King.

'Just a moment,' said the King, 'there is one more thing you have to do.' And he sat and thought and thought about it. 'Find me a ship that will sail on land as well as on water,' he said, finally. 'Then, you can marry the Princess.'

Dummling hurried back to the forest and told the little old man of the impossible task the King had set him.

'I'll never marry the Princess now,' Dummling said, and for once he was not smiling.

'Leave it to me,' said the old man. 'You helped me and, for the sake of your kind heart, I will help you again.'

So he gave Dummling a marvellous ship that could sail on land as well as water. It was a fine vessel with white, silken sails that billowed to and fro in the breeze. On the sea, the ship rose and fell like a great swan on a pond. On the land it moved just as easily, for the little old man had fitted magic wheels to propel it along the roads.

The King was delighted with his ship, for no other King, anywhere, could boast such a thing, and he was happy to give his daughter in marriage to Dummling. He had proved himself a worthy man to marry her.

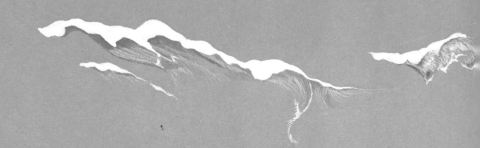

The whole land rejoiced at the wedding celebrations, but Dummling insisted that the guest of honour should be the little, old, grey-bearded man who had helped him. He made him sit at the top table and made sure he was served only the finest wines and the best food.

All the people who had been stuck to the goose came too, and there was singing and dancing for hours till the castle rang with happiness.

In due time, Dummling became King and he was a very good and wise one. He never forgot the little old man of the forest, but though he often looked for him, he never found him again.

# Jack and the Beanstalk

MANY, many years ago, a boy called Jack lived with his mother in a little cottage in the country. They were very poor, and often went hungry, but they did have a Guernsey cow they called Bessie. She was a fine, brown and white animal that gave more milk than any other cow in the neighbourhood. Jack was very proud of her and liked to go to market and sell butter and cheese made from her milk.

One day, his mother called him. She was looking very sad. 'It's no use, Jack,' she said, 'Bessie will have to go. I must pay the rent tomorrow and we have nothing else left to sell. Take her to the market and be sure to get as much money as you can for her.'

Sadly, Jack tied a rope to Bessie's neck and led her along the winding, dusty road to town. Usually, he enjoyed going to the town, especially on market day when the square was busy with stalls, and there were lots of people around. But today he was miserable for he liked Bessie, and he was worried about how they would manage without her.

As he walked along the road in the sunshine, Jack met an old man who asked him where he was taking the cow.

'I'm taking Bessie to market,' said Jack, 'we have no money and my mother has told me to sell her.'

'I'll buy her from you, and save you the trouble of going to market,' said the old man.

'How much will you give me?' said Jack, remembering that his mother had told him to get all the money he could for Bessie.

'I'll give you these beans in exchange for the cow,' said the old man. He opened a small bag and showed Jack the beans. Jack had never seen any beans like these before. There were five of them, all different colours, and they shone in the sunlight.

But he hesitated. What would his mother say if he came home with beans instead of money?

'These are no ordinary beans,' said the old man, 'they are *magic* beans. If you plant them, they will grow up to the sky itself!'

So Jack took the bag of beans and with a final pat, handed Bessie to the old man who led her away. Jack ran home.

'Mother,' he called, 'look what I've got!' And he showed her the bag of beans.

His mother was very angry indeed. 'You gave Bessie away for a bag of beans,' she shouted, 'you stupid boy. Now go to bed. There is no supper for you tonight.' And she wept with despair. Picking up the beans she threw them out of the window. 'What shall we do now?' she cried.

Jack fell asleep feeling very unhappy and very hungry. He woke up early the next morning feeling even more hungry. He hurried into the kitchen to look for some food and an amazing sight met his eyes!

He could see through the window a tall, green stalk climbing up and up, as far as the clouds in the sky. Great, green leaves sprouted like a ladder from top to bottom.

Jack could not wait to see where the stalk went, and, without saying goodbye to his mother, he rushed out of the cottage and started to climb. It took him a long time to reach the very top, but it was worth it. He could see for miles and the sun felt very warm on his head.

He stepped off the beanstalk on to a road that lay in front of him. It went on and on right up to the door of the biggest castle

Jack had ever seen. There was no one about, so he thought he would knock on the door and see if someone would give him some breakfast. His long climb had made him even more hungry and thirsty.

The great oak door was shut, but Jack plucked up his courage and knocked loudly. At last an old woman opened it a crack, and he asked her if she could spare some food as he had not eaten for a long time.

'Come in, come in,' she said, 'you can help with the chickens in return for a meal. But be careful of my husband. If he sees you, he will eat you up!'

She gave Jack some bread and milk, but he had only eaten half of it when he heard a very loud noise.

Bump! Thump! Bump! The walls shook and the floor moved under his feet. Jack trembled, and the milk spilled out of the bowl on to the floor.

'Quick! It's my husband,' said the old woman, 'you must hide. Into the oven with you before he sees you.'

It was dark inside the oven, but Jack peeked out of a tiny crack. A huge giant had come into the room! The giant looked all around him, and shouted,

> 'Fee, fi, fo, fum,
> I smell the blood of an Englishman;
> Be he alive or be he dead,
> I'll grind his bones to make my bread.'

'Nonsense!' said his wife, 'you can smell that ox I have roasted for your breakfast. Sit down and eat it while it is hot.'

Jack had never seen anyone as big as the giant. He watched as the giant stuck his fork into huge pieces of the ox his wife had cooked for him, and the fat ran down his chin. Piece by piece, he ate a whole ox which was more food than Jack and his mother had in a year, and he washed it down with quarts of ale from a barrel at his side. At last he had had enough and he called out to his wife.

'Wife, bring me my magic hen. I want some more of her golden eggs.'

The giant's wife brought in a small, brown hen and put it on the table in front of her husband.

'Lay!' commanded the giant, and to Jack's astonishment, a golden egg fell on to the table. 'More!' said the giant, and soon a pile of golden eggs lay on the cloth in front of him. The giant scooped the eggs into his pocket. Then he lay back in his chair and was soon asleep. His snores were so loud that the plates on the shelf shook with the noise.

Jack crept out of the oven and, tucking the magic hen under his arm, ran as fast as his legs would carry him down the road to the beanstalk.

'Mother!' he called, 'see what I have brought!' And he put the little, brown hen on the table in the cottage and told it to lay. Soon, there was a pile of golden eggs on the table. Jack's mother could not believe her eyes as the eggs shone brightly in the light from the cottage window. She hugged Jack with joy. Now she would be able to pay the rent and buy all the food they needed. They would never be poor again.

After a while, Jack grew restless. He wanted another chance to see the giant and climb the magic beanstalk. He slipped out early, before his mother could stop him, and climbed to the top of the beanstalk. Everything was the same as before, and he lost no time in going up to the castle door. The old woman did not remember him, but she thought he would be useful to her and hid him in a cupboard when she heard the giant coming.

Thump! Bump! Thump! The walls trembled and the floor shook and the giant came into the room.

'*Fee, fi, fo, fum,*
*I smell the blood of an Englishman,*'
he bellowed, but his wife cut him short.

'Rubbish! You have such a cold you cannot smell anything,' she snapped. 'Now do stop all that noise and eat this sheep I've roasted for you.'

Now the only sound that Jack could hear was the giant eating, and piece by piece a whole sheep disappeared down his great throat. Jack was amazed!

When he had finished eating, the giant called out to his wife.

'Wife, bring me the key to my treasure chest.'

The giant's wife brought in an enormous iron key and the giant opened the huge chest standing by the table. It was piled high with bags full of golden coins! Jack watched as the giant counted the coins out into two big sacks.

After such a huge meal, the giant found all this counting very tiring, and he began yawning, and soon lay back in his chair fast asleep. His great snores sounded like thunder. Jack crept from his hiding place and, snatching one of the sacks, ran along the road and slid down the beanstalk.

'Mother! Mother!' he shouted, 'look what I have brought you this time!'

His mother scolded him a little, but she was delighted with the coins. She had never seen so many, and they gave up trying to count them all.

'No more visits to the giant,' she warned Jack, but he only laughed. He wanted to go once more to the giant's castle.

So, next morning, he got up early and climbed to the top of the beanstalk and hurried along the path to the castle. Jack was afraid that the old woman might not let him in again so he crept in through a window and hid behind a huge milk churn.

The walls shook and the floor trembled and Jack knew the giant was coming!

> '*Fee, fi, fo, fum,*
> *I smell the blood of an Englishman.*
> *Be he alive or be he dead,*
> *I'll grind his bones to make my bread.*'

The giant's voice echoed around the room and Jack began to wish that he had listened to his mother and not climbed the beanstalk again. The giant looked in the oven, then he looked in the cupboard, but just as he was getting close to Jack's hiding place, the old woman bustled in.

'What are you doing?' she said crossly. 'Come and eat your breakfast.' So the giant sat down to his breakfast of five roast hens and ten loaves of bread.

When the giant had finished eating, Jack wondered what he would do. After all, he no longer had so much money, or his golden egg laying hen! Jack didn't have long to wait.

'Wife!' shouted the giant, 'open my box of jewels!' The giant's wife opened the huge box and as Jack watched, the giant thrust his hand inside it and took out red rubies that were as dark as blood, sapphires as blue as the sky and diamonds as big as hens' eggs. But the giant soon tired of looking at the jewels, and leaving the box open by his chair, he ordered his wife to bring his harp.

This was the most beautiful harp Jack had ever seen, for it was made of pure and shining gold that sparkled and shimmered as the giant gently plucked the strings. The giant told the harp to play him a lullaby. The soft, sweet music flowed into the room, and soon its gentle sounds were replaced by the giant's snores. He was fast asleep.

Jack crept out once more from his hiding place and snatched some of the jewels. Then he looked at the harp. It was too beautiful to leave behind so he picked it up. But as he touched it, the harp began to call out, 'Master! Master!' The strings twanged and twisted and woke the giant with their noise.

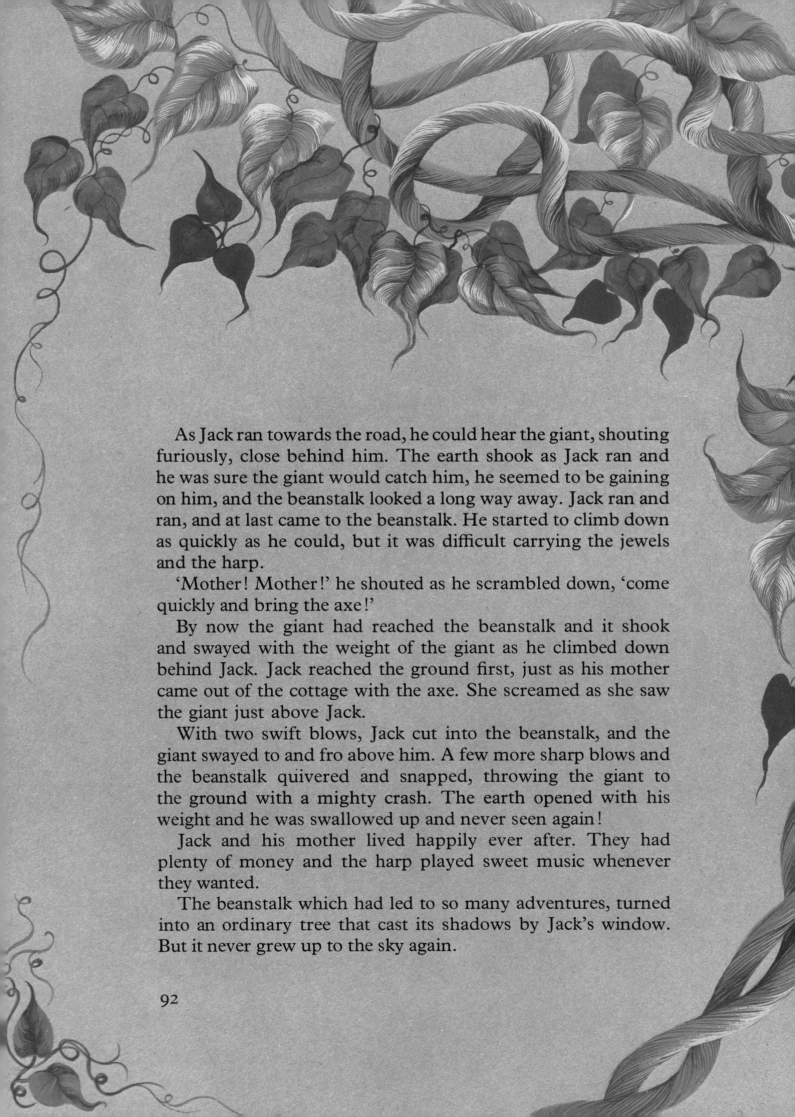

As Jack ran towards the road, he could hear the giant, shouting furiously, close behind him. The earth shook as Jack ran and he was sure the giant would catch him, he seemed to be gaining on him, and the beanstalk looked a long way away. Jack ran and ran, and at last came to the beanstalk. He started to climb down as quickly as he could, but it was difficult carrying the jewels and the harp.

'Mother! Mother!' he shouted as he scrambled down, 'come quickly and bring the axe!'

By now the giant had reached the beanstalk and it shook and swayed with the weight of the giant as he climbed down behind Jack. Jack reached the ground first, just as his mother came out of the cottage with the axe. She screamed as she saw the giant just above Jack.

With two swift blows, Jack cut into the beanstalk, and the giant swayed to and fro above him. A few more sharp blows and the beanstalk quivered and snapped, throwing the giant to the ground with a mighty crash. The earth opened with his weight and he was swallowed up and never seen again!

Jack and his mother lived happily ever after. They had plenty of money and the harp played sweet music whenever they wanted.

The beanstalk which had led to so many adventures, turned into an ordinary tree that cast its shadows by Jack's window. But it never grew up to the sky again.